THE
PLOTINUS

THE
PLOTINUS

Rikki Ducornet

COFFEE HOUSE PRESS
Minneapolis
2023

Coffee House Press books are available to the trade through our primary distributor, Consortium Book Sales & Distribution, cbsd.com or (800) 283-3572. For personal orders, catalogs, or other information, write to info@coffeehousepress.org.

Coffee House Press is a nonprofit literary publishing house. Support from private foundations, corporate giving programs, government programs, and generous individuals helps make the publication of our books possible. We gratefully acknowledge their support in detail in the back of this book.

LIBRARY OF CONGRESS CATALOGING-IN-PUBLICATION DATA

Names: Ducornet, Rikki, 1943– author.
Title: The plotinus / Rikki Ducornet.
Description: Minneapolis : Coffee House Press, 2023.
Identifiers: LCCN 2022055198 (print) | LCCN 2022055199 (ebook) |
   ISBN 9781566896818 (paperback) | ISBN 9781566896825 (epub)
Classification: LCC PS3554.U279 P56 2023 (print) |
   LCC PS3554.U279 (ebook) | DDC 813/.54—dc23
LC record available at https://lccn.loc.gov/2022055198
LC ebook record available at https://lccn.loc.gov/2022055199

PRINTED IN THE UNITED STATES OF AMERICA

30 29 28 27 26 25 24 23   1 2 3 4 5 6 7 8

Glimpses of The Plotinus *surfaced in*
Conjunctions *and* Big Other.
My heartfelt thanks goes to
Brad Morrow and John Madera.

This book is for Mona, Atefeh, and Kristoffer.

The NVLA series is an artistic playground where authors challenge and broaden the outer edges of storytelling. Each novella illuminates the capacious and often overlooked space of possibilities between short stories and novels. Unified by Sarah Evenson's bold and expressive series design, NVLA places works as compact as they are complex in conversation to demonstrate the infinite potential of the form.

THE
PLOTINUS

Agitated and pressed for time, I grabbed the knobby stick—a harmless memento of the footpath—now long gone—that had for a time provided access to the woods (such as they were) and ran into the street unprepared for the inevitable encounter (such a dope!) with the Plotinus. A shriek later and my knobby stick was reduced to dust along with my shoes and socks, my coveralls—these losses accompanied by a blinding light, ear pain impossible to articulate, and my arrest.

Secluded in a closet, its air vent accessible on tiptoe, I relate this in code using my knuckles against the grid to whoever will listen. (Very few can possibly decipher my desperate rappings, but the one who does will be the right one. Even in good times, when we would set off for the woods together with our knobby sticks, to bury the birds as they fell from the sky, we were not many.)

They tell me that my transgressions—if merely phenomenological—are punishable by a public scouring, and so I live each day thankful for what I have, although what I have—apart from my threadbare aspirations—is only the sack. If given a chance, I will request another, not because I like it, but because the one I have—if it conceals my apertures as the Powers would have it—leaves my knees and legs bare. If and when my request is gratified (one must remain hopeful), I will ask for my socks back or, preferably, a new pair. I like to imagine the socks are brought to me in a white cardboard box, and that they are wrapped in white tissue paper stamped with the manufacturer's name: Mothwing. Each night before sleep (such as it is) the box appears as if by enchantment, and I whisper: Here you are! Praise destiny! I open the box very slowly, and I take my time with the paper, too. Sometimes I fall asleep even before I see the socks!

• • •

The first pair of socks I received were yellow—a transgressive color, so like the Sun, so like the yolk of an egg. If it came to be known that I owned a pair of yellow socks, the color of an evil star, of the yolk of an egg— the tangible proof of procreation—it would all be over.

The yellow socks warmed my feet, and that first night I slept until a thin ribbon of light made its way into the closet, awakening me. Looking down at my feet, I saw that the socks were gone—a good thing as had the Vector appeared, he would have seen them at once, and then . . . But this did not happen. The socks are programmed to dissolve at the break of light; a mere whisper is enough to stimulate their dissolution. (I do not know if in the long run the process will adversely affect my feet.) Between you and me, things would be so much better all around if I could keep the socks *and* be provided with a second sack.

• • •

I can never tell when the Vector will show up, for he moves about cloaked in his Ginza and treading air. His aversion to the Sun is so great he wears two Ginzas, one on his body (such as it is) and one on his head. This makes for an impressive entry. Always he asks that I remove my sack so that he may look upon my scars— each one corresponding to an evil deed. The first time this occurred I pointed out that the scars had been inflicted arbitrarily by the Plotinus on that fateful morning when I left the house (such as it was) with the knobby stick. Until then I had not a scab to my name. Now when the Vector pops in, I attempt to flatter him and then, once primed, use what is left of my wits to suggest that like the cold white Moon, my scars provide a key to a vast cosmical system that, once unraveled, will reveal that like a painted turtle, my body provides a map that leads directly to the Throne of Memory. I am, I tell him, like the berry bush that, long ago in the depths of winter, provided sweetness to the birds seeking sustenance in blizzards. As gullible as a cracker pigeon, the Vector, his eyes swelling with tears, falls to his knees when I speak like this. I bid him rise.

• • •

I awoke from a place in my mind thinking how very odd it is that as I regress and shrink into myself (what is left of it), beyond my closet there are corridors, there are other closets, tens of thousands, perhaps, a vast surgical theater (or so it is rumored) patrolled by the Plotinus whose other assigned tasks are to assure my breakfast and that the Vector's attentions are timely and scrutable. Should the Vector bring a sack to an incarcerate, say, he would have to secure it somehow beneath his Ginza in such a way as to fudge the pokeabout.

But! Be this as it may, I have been thinking in my mind (such as it is) that beyond all this misery, my own and that of the multitude of others, each and every one an incarcerate too, exists the vast world (or what remains of it) and its Moon—a Moon as pocked as I am yet unlike me, swarming with activity on both its dark and luminous faces. And in my mind's thinking it has come to me that although it is shameful without end to be thus reduced, I once (and not so long ago, either) was the one Beauty acknowledged in the world with a look, yes: she looked upon me and smiled.

• • •

At times, my ear straining beneath the vent, I witness conversations taking place on the other side, on a street or a balcony, perhaps, or a porch—considering my daily dose of sunlight. In the recent past I heard a woman or a child ask for mercy only to be told in no uncertain terms that there is no mercy to be had in this universe—a thing I pondered and will continue to ponder. My conclusion (such as it is thus far) is that if it is so, that there is no mercy in this universe, there may be mercy elsewhere. For it is rumored that the number of universes is infinite, that each is a portal to the next. It occurs to me as I knuckle the grid that if true, well, then, perhaps they inform one another in ways both nefarious and beneficial. (Such conjectures got me through the day's interminable dusk and much of the night.)

And what if each thing both inanimate and animate is a portal to the next thing and so to all things?

• • •

Today (such as it is) I tidied up the closet by sweeping the floor clear of dust with my feet. This afforded exercise and a certain satisfaction; it was a pleasure to see the dust piled up in one corner looking very like a small hillock. I squatted squinting and imagined that I was looking at a distant mountain at dusk and that it had snowed. I imagined that the Vector dropped by with the second sack, that the Plotinus had allowed him to enter, that the sack covered my legs and knees, that the Vector had given me a rope to tie the sack in place and, what's more, a pair of socks, that these socks were yellow, as yellow as the yolk of the maligned egg, the egg that is considered horrible, that is unsound. In doing this, the Vector had broken all the rules. He had risked his own coherence and contiguousness.

The Vector whispered that the Plotinus was only able to see out of one eye, so that the pokeabout had been compromised and he had passed through without a hitch! I hid the socks beneath the precious mound of dust that, as the Sun declined in the sky beyond the air vent, mysteriously glowed, giving off a soft, golden light.

If I had a twig, I said, a small twig sporting maybe a leaf or two, well then, a moment's dreaming and it would contain all the splendors, the raptures and the mysteries of the world. Like Adam's, I continued, my isolation is my innocence.

I happen to have a twig hidden within the folds of my Ginza, the Vector murmured, as he burrowed into a pocket so deep I assumed it contained any number of things, and, indeed, as if conjured by magic, out came the laurel twig, three bright green leaves clinging to its summit. The closet would soon be submerged in darkness, but before this happened, we got to see the tree proudly rooted at the summit of the snowy mound. I cannot express the gratitude I felt for the Vector then, nor the extent of my happiness.

We were now submerged in darkness; the Vector had neglected his watch. Now that it is night, I said to him, just knowing the tree on its hill is there, I shall pass the hours in peace. Bowing, the Vector backed out into the hallway and vanished.

Soon after the Vector's departure, the Plotinus came clanging down the hallway, its lights flashing and siren nozzle screeching. It raged into my closet, kicked the snowy mound and stomping on the twig reduced it to pieces. Once it had rolled on, with morning far away, there was nothing to do but sit on my knees still as a stone and consider the positive aspects of exile and of my diminished circumstances.

• • •

This morning (such as it was), my breakfast was a hard roll, very like a rock; despite my youth I feared it was a tooth smasher, and, indeed, it remained intact even after being hurled at the cruel walls with force. At some point I got to my knees, set it down on the tiled floor and considered the very real possibility that the object before me was not a breakfast roll but a rock. I decided that this could be used to my advantage as it offered the possibility of a systematic inquiry into brute matter. I had—if some time ago—studied Theophrastus (in eighth grade, such as it was, with Botword) and so know that stones are divided into two main classes: stones and earths. I also considered a third possibility, that the thing before me *had been* a breakfast roll and was now a fossil. Therefore, I began my inquiry by putting the thing to my nose and inhaling. I smelled nothing but my own smell and this provided no comfort. For this I decided to be grateful. Had the thing offered an atom of the dairy, the oven, or the kitchen, surely my heart (such as it is) would have broken. Yet, risking this, not long after, I sniffed at it again, thoughtfully, taking my time—so that, inevitably, I began to brood on the distant past, when each home had its hearth, its pantry and a kitchen that—if only on special occasions (and this before Clampdown)—smelled of butter and yeast. And I recalled the poached eggs of antiquity, that subversion,

that obscenity, the egg swelling from within its muf-
fin, incubating beneath its blanket of cream sauce. The
sacred egg that would one day grow wings, rise to the
skies and sing (as, believe it or not, was once the case,
for yes, in antiquity the skies were schooled with birds).

• • •

Theophrastus insisted that all stones *are formed from
some pure and homogeneous matter.* When I look at the
thing I ascertain that it *is not pure.* And I cannot know
if it is homogeneous without breaking it. Theophrastus
goes on to say that this homogeneous nature is *the result
of a conflux or percolation.* (The same could be said of a
breakfast roll.) All I have to abrade my rock's shell and
in this way continue my investigations are the nails of
my fingers and toes. (I refuse to compromise what is left
of my teeth.)

• • •

Sometime later I heard the Plotinus on its way back
(and this could not have been more fortunate) with a
jar of water capped with a cork. As soon as the Plotinus
had moved on, I dropped my rock into the water jar.
What happened next was momentous. The rock dissolved and in this way provided sustenance of a kind—
even if I still had no clue as to its true nature.

Having breakfasted (as best I could), I considered the day's gifts—the rock that had proved to be a breakfast roll of a kind; the water (and so a broth that would now sustain me for a time); the silent breath of sunlight leaking from the vent; the vent's percussive capacities; the fact of a floor that, if cold and hard, was dry; the extraordinary luck that the shithole had a cover of sorts and that this cover was carefully considered by its manufacturer—a thing all too rare. Then I sat on my knees and considered the possibility that the Sun was greeting me as best it could considering its limited access.

Then, when the Sun's breath vanished and the night claimed the closet, I, grateful for the magic water, remained on my knees and, bending over, continued where the vanished rock left off. Theophrastus wrote: *Some stones can be melted and others cannot; some can be burnt and others cannot . . . And some, like the Smaragdos, can make the color of water the same as their own.* In other words, my rock was named Smaragdos.

• • •

All was quiet and I was quiet; I remained on my knees forever and a day—or so it seemed—as still as a body can be, doubled over just as a rock that has been tested by fire folds upon itself, just as the brain forming within its bone is the child of enfoldment. At some point I got to my feet, and knuckling the air vent *was stung by a hornet.* At that very moment, the Vector—and his name is Furanus—appeared; Furanus, a corruption of the name Furmastic (the tyrant of the myth of Cordplaster who bore witness to the birth of the Moon). For a time we squatted together in silence. If the floor is cold, it is also filthy.

Master, the Vector startled me with this greeting, I have brought you yet another gift. Poking about the depths of his Ginza, he eventually nabbed a small glass jar, and with ceremonious attitude, handed it over. Inside was a piece of fresh honeycomb, the color of the Sun itself. As the keeping of bees is punishable by death, I looked into his eyes, inquiringly.

I live, Furanus, told me, far from men in a valley where there remains a vast stand of lime trees. When he said this, I could see the valley and its trees, and for a brief moment I thought I could smell the lime trees in blossom, could hear the gentle buzzing of the bees. Furanus handed over a spoon. As there was no way I could hide the jar from the Plotinus, I had no choice but to eat the comb at once. After a spoonful of that honey, wax falling apart between my teeth, I wept, awakened from the dry well in which I had been living to be deposited in a sunlit valley. I could not stop weeping, although I feared that at any moment the Plotinus would appear and Furanus and I would be torn to pieces. When I caught my breath I said: You have provided the last pleasure I will ever know, for by the time the Sun breathes into my air vent, I will have turned to stone. Deep into the well of my ear, the Vector muttered: Inevitably.

• • •

This evening, rain fell in a purple light giving way to hail, and, later, a heavy fog of dust. Our sons are endangered by betrayals, the Vector had said to me once before departing. What am I saying? Even before they are born!

• • •

With little to occupy my thoughts, I am a keen observer of the self's decline. (As is said: The floaters dissolve, revealing the beloved's face, the mole on her cheek.)

• • •

There is a hum within my head as within a hive bereft of its queen. An angry hum. The companion of my solitude, it provides a white noise of a kind; it is like a broom. My anger is rooted in my losses. The loss of my knobby stick, the path that led to the woods (such as they were), the loss of those diminutive graves we cared for. (Sometimes a bird would fall alone; other times an entire flock would rain down from the sky. Nonetheless, the Beauty and I would give each one its own place to rest, each resting place marked by a stone.)

• • •

Sometimes I think that had I a honey drop I could suck on, I would be happy, would need nothing else. A rock needs nothing, yet a little sweetness is not a bad thing. One lives, after all, for pleasure. Pleasure happens, the Beauty once told me, laughing. Gently nibbling on the open palm of my hand.

• • •

Today the Sun was of such force it tore into the vent and collided with the back wall where it settled for not a negligible time. I could tell by its magnitude that the Sun was facing my way, that its back was not turned on me as the Plotinus had insisted the day of my arrest. It was and is always my conviction that the Sun and Moon do not turn away from us, but look upon us with benevolence. That light, as it is intended, benefits those who dwell upon a planet made of rock and fire. It is known that our Moon and Sun are by nature wanderers yet choose to stay near us, as they know we need the light to withstand the terrible rigors of loneliness. It does not matter that the Moon is fickle, first scowling and then beaming. Unlike the Sun, which recedes only to return. (I am telling you nothing new.) The Moon shrinks only to swell. (It is thought with seawater.) This swelling of the Moon allows me to swell; as it wanes, so do I wane. When the Sun rises, so do I rise. When the day is as dark as ashes, so am I dark.

I await, somewhat breathlessly, news from Mars, should this news reach the public. My question is: Will the Sun and Moon turn to face those who look up from the Martian soil, or will they keep their backs turned? I will question the Vector when he reappears. I will ask him to keep up with the rumors as they surface. There is never a paucity of rumors! I was taught that the planets hang like fruit from a tree, that the motion they make is caused by a wind generated by the gods in conflict and in conversation. This verity is outdone however by troublesome rumors. Just prior to my arrest, it was whispered in the streets that those who went to the Martian Lamp were in no way impeded by a branch or a string.

I was taught that some lamps burn oil and others fuel themselves. I would like to know if the Mars Lamp is made of fire or clay or a luminous dust. I am well aware that asking such questions is unwise. If I could, I would ask Gazali. If there were still astronomers, I would ask them. But the Vector is the only one I have, and he has, after all, proved a sympathetic witness to my sorry state; he appears to approve my mission to become a fully integrated saturate of self. To become a thing that knows nothing beyond *what it is*. (The Vector appears to think of me as one who has a sacred mission, who knows more than I know. I know nothing.)

• • •

Sometime later in the day, knuckling the vent, once again I was stung, stung to the quick on my thumb so that the swelling compromises this telling—yet I persist. For if thus far the conversation is one-sided, still it is ripe with possibility, its outcome unknown.

The question of the day is: Have I been horneted (as it were) by the same hornet or not? These digressions—the knuckling, the horneting—disrupt my intentional project: to fossilize in place. For the pain in my thumb has awakened me to the fact that my body is the vessel of my mind and so myself.

• • •

Restless in the night I recalled a poem my mother recited before she put me to sleep:

> Do you not see how the fish
> Swallow the burning stars
> So that we may get on with
> Our evening?
> So that we may get on with
> Our dreaming?

• • •

Today (such as it was) in a pool of light the size of a thumbnail, I found a saffron-complexioned hornet on the floor, barely moving. Although it was surely she who had stung me twice, still I was entranced by the sight of a living thing on the floor beside me and in need of my attentions. I searched the floor centimeter by centimeter to see if by chance a crumb of sweet wax had fallen there, and sure enough, within a moment, I found a crumb big enough to excite a hornet's interest. Very slowly and making what I hoped was a reassuring murmuration, a cross between a droning or a buzzing and a purring, I managed to approach her and to position this crumb before her face, a face with eyes of such intensity I felt their fire burn into mine. Slowly, and with unexpected grace, she approached the crumb and, with a paw, gave it a gentle knock so that it rolled closer. A trace of honey sparkled in what remained of the day's light.

I noticed that her body was striped with amber, and that her eyes were the color of blue apothecary bottle glass. A cobalt blue threaded with gold. Her face is elegant. She has what was once called a frimousse, meaning an irresistible, somewhat feline look: good cheekbones and a delicate, nicely proportioned chin. My beloved's face was like this; she, too, had a frimousse, and I could not help but find myself deeply taken with this tiny creature that is—as I am still—sentient. I could tell that this was so by the way her eyes met mine, the way she prodded the wax with her little paw, the way she tilted her head this way and that, the way she gazed at the crumb only to then gaze upon me, then back at the crumb once again. In this way the day passed into night. Its arrival was sudden, as if a lid had come crashing down upon us. As carefully as I could, I turned away from her so as not to frighten her and, afraid that I might unwittingly harm her in my sleep, remained awake and vigilant throughout the night.

• • •

Morning came in this way: something like a tear of light appeared just beneath the air vent; the vent itself was not visible; the tear descended further and then became a smudge; over the minutes the smudge solidified, gathered a certain muscle and heft, and all at once became a bright octagon. At this moment in time, the Sun swarmed the vent, providing one bright rectangle, bright enough to illuminate the sleeping hornet who lay comfortably extended, her amber, ebony, and gold marvelous to see. Her eyes were closed, and the crumb? The crumb was gone. Instant by instant, as safely as I could, I walked to the pitcher and dipped my finger in the water. Returning to her with a wet finger, I let a drop or two fall a centimeter or so from her face. Her eyes opened then, and when she gazed into mine, every nerve in my body awakened to a delicious stinging, banishing each and every thought I had had and might have had about intentional fossilization. Then she stood up.

The movement she made was somewhere between that of a cat and a camel. That is to say, her bottom rose first and as it ascended so did she stretch out her front quarters, her little arms and paws reaching out before her. I noticed how slender her legs are (she has six!); they could not be trimmer. And her paws! They could not be more delicate.

Theophrastus said that *some stones are rare and small, such as the Smaragdos*. It came to me that as my hornet was (surely) rare and as she was small, I should name her Smaragdos, so I did.

Smaragdos! I murmured. The day has begun, and it is ours! The Vector will come, and when he does, I will request more honeycomb as I see you have polished off the crumb as I intended. Smaragdos then bowed her head, and closing her eyes as if in expectation of delight, stuck out her tongue, a tongue as delicate as a silk thread, and lapped up the little pool of water.

• • •

At some point or other during the morning, and after she had breakfasted, Smaragdos took off through the air vent and I continued with my account of things (such as they are). The Plotinus neglected to bring me breakfast, and so when the Vector showed up, I was nearly delirious with gratitude. For one thing he had brought two breakfast rolls tucked away in his Ginza and studded with raisins. And! As I had dreamed, another little jar of honeycomb appeared an instant after. This morning I breakfasted like a king. I secreted the second roll within my uppermost sack where it would provide not only tomorrow's meal, but a little warmth. (It had just come from the baker's!) I was uncertain if I could risk sharing with the Vector my good news about having a companion named Smaragdos; I also feared to speak of her out loud might compromise my luck and she might never return. I said nothing, but thinking of her all the while was careful to drop a good sized crumb of wax to the floor, for despite my fears, I was optimistic, certain she would be back, that the stinging I had felt when our eyes met, she had felt, too.

. . .

Are you, I asked the Vector, familiar with the words of Theophrastus?

It is not safe to speak of Theophrastus, the Vector whispered, but . . . the Plotinus is currently under repair (or so I have been told), having collided with a second Plotinus in the corridor. Both are under repair, he added, his whispering grating on my ear like sandpaper.

I have been thinking about Theophrastus myself, he added, for yesterday a house was burned down along with its library and an exemplary collection of pottery. As the fire was immensely hot, the pottery exploded, creating a terrific ruckus in the neighborhood. When later I heard what had happened, I recalled what Theophrastus said about the many stones which break and fly into pieces as if they are fighting against being burnt—like pottery, for example.

It has puzzled me, I said to the Vector, that Theophrastus would speak of pottery but a moment after speaking of true stones such as the Smaragdos! As I said this my heart leapt, for never had I expected to have such a conversation with anyone, locked away as I was in my closet! And it leapt—need I say it—because I had found a way to say her name *out loud*—not to myself, but to the Vector, another person entirely. (Or so I presume.)

• • •

After the Vector left, things became stranger. In some ways they became better because I could no longer hear the dreadful racket the Plotinus made when it raged through the corridors, up and down, back and forth. But I did hear a commotion somewhere far away in the streets and at the same time, the pleading on the porch (or balcony?) beside me worsened. There was also a fair amount of smoke coming through my air vent—a thing I should have the right to complain about. And I feared for my beloved Smaragdos, for I knew the smoke would offend her as well. I also heard explosions and supposed more pottery was losing its battle with fire.

This digression reminds me that just when I had the chance to ask the Vector as to the nature of what lies on the other side of the wall, I forgot.

• • •

All day (such as it is) I wait planted in one spot so that I may scrutinize the air vent. Again and again my thoughts return to that moment of moments when my beloved, her tongue a thread of silk, appears as if on fire and of a sudden—as does a falling star. When she does appear (it must happen!), a sky studded with dead planets will once again be hung with mirrors.

I have resolved that when she reappears, I will greet her with my eyes and direct my gaze (and so her own) to the crumb and its pond. I will look on in a fever as she paws the crumb and tongues the water.

• • •

It comes to me, after a day on my feet, that truth is *not* found in consequences (i.e., my restless waiting) but, in this current moment at least—is the *cause* of consequences (my restless waiting). The truth is the moment Smaragdos's tongue prods the crumb. (This gesture is ambiguous.)

• • •

My beloved's eyes are like candles of camphor.

• • •

Smaragdos is not a hornet as much as she is a fairy.

• • •

My night was mired in perplexity. My second sack had vanished—an impossibility as none but the Vector and nothing but the Plotinus—now too compromised to travel—could enter my closet. Not only that! My second breakfast roll, the one that had given me such unaccustomed warmth, had vanished as well. I am certain I had not eaten it. Vividly, I recall my decision to keep it for the morning. There was nothing to do but search the closet's every corner (all four of them) in the dark, taking care not to disturb the previous crumbs until the roll revealed itself; it did not. Nor did the

yellow socks, which mattered to me as much, exist any-where within reach. I spent the night on my knees, a mad hope in my heart, and then, when the Sun came up (a thing I am unable to actually witness), I stared into each and every corner, only to once again find nothing. The crumb, too, remained unscrutable, but at least I knew it was there; my eyesight, never very good, has, or so it seems, been further compromised by my unrelenting seclusion. (I have lost all notion of time, such as it is.)

• • •

Today I returned to my position beneath the air vent, as is my custom, to continue my coded rapping. After all, this activity has precipitated my quickening, the assurance that despite evidence to the contrary, *life is happening!* I know I risked a sting; I longed for that sting. Smaragdos's sting rings my bell; its vibrations—so like the fluids emanating from the Sun and Moon— assure that the moments proceed rather than sink into one another.

• • •

Living under diminished circumstances (to put it mildly) means that one is apt to make mistakes of judgment. Today I did just that. I spoke to the Vector about Smaragdos, her beauty, and the stings she had inflicted. Told him that her stings had precipitated a quickening, the assurance that life continues to happen. I told him that Smaragdos' sting is like the ringing of a bell, that its vibration (how it rocked my entire being!) is akin to the fluids emanating from the Sun and Moon; her sting assures a feeling of instantaneity—a feeling I have not felt for many months or longer; years, perhaps. Her sting's reverberations flood a body with light; they illumine the heart and mind. I told him of her fairy ways, how I looked on with admiration as she prodded the crumb with a grace, the likes of which I had never seen.

All I desire, I said to the Vector, is to witness such beauty each day—even if at a certain distance. (It is true that all I have ever desired of the world is beauty, yet I have been mightily punished for this desire.)

Until that moment, the Vector had looked upon me with something like awe, even affection. But now he appeared to rise above me like a hydraulic lift, to take on height and heft. His visage veered rufulus and his mood erupted.

To love an animal, he scolded, is as hateful as loving a member of one's own sex. It is abhorrent in the eyes of the Archons, the heart of the Hierophant, the mind of the Vectory, the souls of the planets, the ears of the Mantis. When the Mantis hears of such madness, his ears bleed. For it is said:

> *The one who lusts for the hornet*
> *buggers the beardless youth.*

But! I began . . . The Vector turned away, his face frozen to the opposite wall. But! Don't you see? I attempted, addressing the back of his Ginza. This was too much for the Vector who had already vanished, as if in a puff of smoke, never to return.

• • •

The Vector gone, there was no hope for breakfast, let alone conversation. The Vector be damned, I thought, the Mantis be damned. I returned to my position beneath the vent, and with my knuckles continued my narration with something like a vengeance, thinking of the possible pleasures ahead as well as the risks. Such considerations were abruptly canceled by a harrowing sting, followed by the sudden encounter with a hornet at least three times the size of Smaragdos who had come to settle accounts. In no time he had toured my closet, polished off the honeyed crumb, and, his wings ferociously buzzing, helicoptered in place an inch from my nose all the while threatening me with his eyes.

• • •

I spent the night famished and scolding myself. For a time I would scold myself, and then I would imagine the things I would order if there had been a way to order takeout. Before I knew it, I was wandering Fred's Grocery, that church of absolute and authentic good, its unfailing magnitude, its everlasting qualities extending in all directions simultaneously and never depleted, never knowing exhaustion.

When morning came, my misery was unrelenting still, for I knew the day ahead offered nothing but solitude unrelenting. I would not see Smaragdos again, I would not see the Vector, I doubted I would see the

Plotinus ever again. It was rumored it was in bad shape and, in the words of the Vector, replaceable parts were nonexistent. But then, sometime early in the afternoon, a Novel Plotinus appeared silently on rubber wheels to hand me an object I had never actually seen (but had heard about somewhere or other) called The Frozen Taco. It *was* terribly cold and at first I thought it was an ice cream sandwich. When I bit into a frozen pickle I was disabused. The taco came with a small envelope of hot sauce that had expired in a previous century. This I rubbed on my swollen thumb. And then the unexpected happened.

It was already dark when somewhere deep in the bowels of the facility, a light appeared. This light was bearing down on me. Indeed, within moments, the Novel Plotinus wearing a headlamp, appeared rattling his keys. Before I knew what was happening, a new Vector, or Vectoress, rather, stood before me. Despite the fact that it was hard to see anything clearly, I could see that she was beautiful, her eyebrows unusually splendid and her nostrils as delicate as those of an insect. The moment we were alone, she pulled a box of halva out from under her Ginza. Her name was Jane.

I know, she said, of the trouble you caused with the Vector, and I have come, and will continue to come, in his stead. His hatred of the animal kingdom and of all things feminine is notorious. As I know a thing or two about his own weaknesses . . . she took a breath and whispered: The Mantis—I have his promise that you will not be prosecuted. She then poked around beneath her Ginza and handed me a cold fizzy drink. Seeing my excitement (I believe I was panting) she popped it open before handing it over. I had not had fresh water for days, so you can well imagine how much this meant to me. It was something from the brand Past Time called Tumerzip. It tasted terrific. So terrific something deep in my brain popped open and incandesced.

I am here, the Vectoress continued, as a friend. I have also brought you a supply of honey. It is in an invisibility bottle—I wish I could tell you how I managed *that*! And it comes with its own spoon. Having tasted of the crumb—and yes, the Vector told me everything—Smaragdos will likely return the instant you open the jar.

Having reassured me in this way, she left me, but not without promising to return the following night. (The Vectoress is only allowed mobility at night.) Before her departure, she secreted the empty soda can within her Ginza. As I have no furnishings, I did very much wish I could have held onto it.

As soon as the Vectoress was gone, I cautiously opened the box of halva. The wrapping was clean, and the halva, pistachio, somehow fresh and moist. I dug into it with my little spoon, recalling the words of a prophet: halva is the most noble of pleasures. I could tell right away that it had come from Fred's. This got me thinking, if sporadically, of Fred's all day.

• • •

At the time of my arrest, Fred's was the only grocery left in the universe. Even then the place was more like a museum than a grocery. For example, it had cans of sardines that had fossilized, and a slice of Egyptian cheese over seven thousand years old.

• • •

Fred's grocery was unique in its attempt to create a space in which to contemplate things, from the handsome pyramidal cheeses made from the milk of camels to the cones of sugar. It was a place, perhaps the only place in the known universe, quiet enough, its inventory inventive enough, its star-studded ceiling beautiful enough to provide an atmosphere in which to ponder the nature of things. It was at Fred's sitting on a barrel of nuts that I came to understand that an egg puts itself together as thoughtfully as a crystal.

• • •

How I wish I could look out the vent and see the planets in all their variety and in motion. Then I could appreciate their beauty, and at the same time, acquire a far clearer sense of time's passage.

• • •

Some time ago, I attempted to share thoughts such as these with the Vector, who warned me that if I continued such speculating alone in my closet *aloud*, I risked being swallowed whole by the quicksand of monody. I replied that although this may well be true, silence is a far greater threat than quicksand. When the Vector heard this, he whispered into my ear, his breath's stink searing what remained of my capacities. He said: According to the Law, the persistent monologist shall lose his head. You must know, he added maliciously, that it is evident to everyone: he already has.

It is easy to lose a head, I replied, when arrested on one's stoop and thrashed within an inch of one's life for stepping out holding a knobby stick. If I practiced silence in solitude, I might as well turn to stone. He reminded me that only recently had I considered this seriously. As Smaragdos had rekindled my fire, I had forgotten about it.

When one is a monologist, I continued, one cannot help but monologize, and so despite these warnings, I went on to say that as all things both inert and not are inevitably in contemplation, one day each and every one will awaken aware within its form, knowing

it is the idealization of an idea! Then and then only will all things come together in a point of blinding light, ignite, explode and scatter. Once this scattering comes to a standstill, all things will start over again.

There cannot be a scattering in the mind of the Mantis! the Vector shrieked, stamping his feet and causing the fire alarm to go off and the sprinkler system overhead to send a violent shower of water down upon us. The Vector fled my closet drenched, as I, tearing the sack from my body, used it like a loofah to rub myself down in a deluge that lasted a good twenty minutes. The night proved cold and damp, but in the morning I stood beneath the vent and felt the Sun worm its way through to settle on my cranium, my neck and shoulders. In this way I spent the day (such as it was). I could not stop shivering, but I was spotless. My mood soaring, it came to me that the world (as I imagined it) had come together, or at the very least was coming together, or would, perhaps with luck, come together, and that if it did not, at the very least I was renewed (if hungry and needing a night's sleep). By tomorrow, I thought, I will be as prepared as a man can be to greet his beloved in the light (such as it will be), should she return, surfing the rays of the morning Sun.

• • •

But now! This morning (such as it is) I realize that the shower I had taken yesterday was *before* yesterday, before any number of yesterdays, but not *too many* as, after all, Smaragdos had come into my life only recently. (Of this I am certain.) I wondered aloud what it was I could do, alone as I was, standing in a dark and damp place wearing a sack, longing for my beloved with nothing at hand with which to enchant her. I was like a bowerbird abandoned on a glacier. But then I recalled a magazine article I read in my youth, an old article but wise, that lay on our street in the rain as if it had been intended for me. The article was titled: Celestial Man and the Power of Positive Thinking.

The gist of the article was: The world is tricked out with snares and dubious distractions. Sooner or later it is inevitable that one will fall on bad times. But if you can muster the necessary pluck and spunk, the ambition and the imagination, if you have the proficience, the competence and preparedness, the qualifiedness and credentials, then the universe will open its arms for you, and you will proceed with vigor in safety, a lucky star forever orbiting your head top.

I recall being excited by this discovery, excited by its message of hope, but I was also struck by the words: head top. Perhaps the article had been translated from another language, yet I could not help but continue reading.

Turning the page over, I saw that the article continued on its backside, ending with an advertisement for a pill named PROFICIENCE. (Later, when I spoke to the Beauty about it, she said: My dearest, you fool, do you not understand we are made helpless so that fortunes may be made on pills? Use your head top my love, she added, mussing my hair with her little hand.) I should add that the article continued in this way: The gods will direct you to Luck's portal, you will ignore the son of Chaos who guards its gates, you will acknowledge but bypass the angels of the interior Heavens, and take the stairs (or maybe a ladder, who knows; perhaps they pass out wings)—all the way to the . . . (the rest was unclear having been submerged in mud).

• • •

Recalling all these things, I stood alone tied to a wheel of inescapable questions: What had become of the sack the Vector had brought me, the socks? What had become of the honey the Vectoress had given me in an invisible jar? I could not escape the wheel, although I did everything I could to follow the instructions Gazali had given me so very long ago (or so it seems) on how to imagine my mind as a bird. You may choose a gull or a raven, he said, a falcon, a parrot, or a flamingo. The point is not the bird but to fly unrestrained by Space or Time. Beauty informs the vast universe with grace and with intention, he said; worlds are in harmonious conversations with one another; the stars are ecstatic realms, each one a well-trimmed lamp, giving off a steady light, quivering in the vastness of everlasting possibility.

And then it happened. Or, rather, the Vectoress happened. I mean to say that, her beauty ablaze, her eyebrows the shadow side of the crescent Moon, she appeared of a sudden. I had not heard her coming, no Plotinus lit the way, nor had I realized how dark it was. I had spent the entire day on my feet, in my one sack, upbraiding myself, thinking out loud: I qualify! Do I qualify? What if I do not qualify?

The Vectoress stood before me, her beauty luminous, as if she were herself a moon, a sun, an entire galaxy.

Opening her arms, her Ginza unfurling like the wings of a butterfly, she embraced me, and holding me close to her heart, as Beauty had in another life, said: Rest assured, you qualify. It is the world that does not qualify.

• • •

After the Vectoress departed, I lay on my back and attempted to sleep. She had brought no gifts, but so great was my joy in seeing her, I was not aware of this until after she was gone. I thought that if my mind were a raven, I would sleep and I would dream. And I did.

• • •

FIRST DREAM

• • •

Incandescent and wearing a Ginza of cotton candy, the Vectoress manifested and before vanishing, handed me a sandwich, a Trideck—Fred's most famous sandwich. The Trideck's framework is pickles and Swiss, mango, and a subtle allusion to butter. (In other words, the Four Principles have been adhered to.) Expect an encounter with grilled meats, rice vinegar, lettuce, lime, fish sauce, followed by a brazen intrusion of hummus, falafel, and lamb sausage. Coleslaw, mayo, and fried oysters command the center; egg salad and sliced tomato announce the finish. (The entire sandwich expels an irresistible aroma of the diner and the souk.) The bread that holds it all together is riddled with lunar hollows and depths all pooled with tahini. Did I say that its juices are benevolent and warming? In other words, the one who holds the sandwich in his bony fingers, holds pleasure; he holds ecstasy. When the Trideck dissolved in my hands, I cried out and awakening, summoned the raven and dreamed again.

• • •

SECOND DREAM

• • •

I dreamed I walked in the woods with Beauty and that we saw Gazali perched on a high branch of a tree, offering a diamond bracelet to a raven—the last of its kind. Gazali told us the raven's nest glittered with jewels stolen from a house beyond the city limits, a house on a hill surrounded by a wall of fire and belonging to the Mantis. The bracelet had fallen from the raven's beak, and Gazali was returning it. We saw the raven pluck the bracelet from Gazali's fingers, and then we saw the raven bow.

• • •

THIRD DREAM

• • •

I dreamed again. I was walking down the aisles of
Fred's Grocery admiring the well-stocked shelves, taking note of my favorite things, each one just beyond
my grasp. I especially admired a vast array of exotic
fruit, and reaching for a kiwi, saw that it was glowing
as if electrified—and then, to the sound of crystals on
strings colliding in the wind, everything began to glow,
to buckle and shake; every can, bottle, jar, melon, crate
of oranges, box of eggs glowed, expanded, imploded,
broke apart, dissolved, reassembled into fantastic geo-
metric solids for which there was no name, as the floors
fell away swallowed by the night, and the ceiling's glass
stars were scattered across the sky; I saw mountains of
parrots exploding like rockets, tantrums of eagles, estu-
aries of lions, blue torrents of magpies, a ruin of wrens; I
saw the river of death rising to the Moon, entire alpha-
bets shattering like glass.

• • •

This morning as the sunlight reached the grate and bathed the closet with a soft luminescence, the color of the flesh of a ripe melon, somewhere between orange and pink, I wondered about the nature of the days, the mysterious arrivals and departures of the Vector, the Vectoress, Smaragdos's stunning manifestations. I wondered about the nature of this ongoing and riddling magic, why beauty and wonder come into my closet only to vanish, to be replaced by an absence, a void in my mind, my belly and heart. This void, I realized in a sudden rage, was named Hunger, a hunger so unbearable that I began to shout for the Novel Plotinus (as I knew the old Plotinus was no more in service). I shouted with all my breath that I was hungry, I was thirsty, I was terribly cold, that I needed another sack and socks and something other than the floor to sleep on. I needed these things now, not sooner or later; I needed them NOW! And then I broke apart and sobbed and said to myself, as there was no one to hear me: I want to know what there is beyond the air vent. Another closet? But one with a window? A porch or a balcony? An alley, a public street? I have every right to know! *I must know where the light that comes through the air vent comes from!*

In the silence that followed, a terrible thought came to me. What if I were no longer on planet Earth? What if the Plotinus had taken me to Saturn and had left me there? I was certain I had been abandoned on Saturn, for it was dark and mean, defined by lack and torpor.

I knew it was Saturn because no one came to sit beside me, to ask me what I needed, or about the things I had seen—such as Beauty awakening in the morning and, naked as a mollusk without its shell, walking to her mirror to put on a pair of earrings. Such as Gazali entertaining a raven with songs no one else remembered. If asked, I would tell anyone who would listen that I had fallen, as do all men, from the sky (women never fall entirely to earth); that on the way I was burned by the Sun's fire and made cold by the Moon's icy mirror. And then I was howling for my life. And then, but an instant later, Smaragdos tore through the air vent like a rocket and landed on the floor.

I got down on my knees and, as if on a field of green grass, stretched out beside her, my head in the crook of my hand, so that I could gaze upon her frimousse at leisure, drink the sparkling indigo of her many eyes. For a time I remained glued to the spot barely breathing, but then words tumbled from my mouth as if by magic, each word a rabbit leaping from the void for the stars. Smaragdos, I said, in your gaze I awaken. I am flesh again, no longer stone. Smaragdos, I said. I quicken! At these words I could see her eyes (all five of them) soften. And I could see, despite her diminutive size, that she was smiling. Of a sudden she was on my nose exploring it with tender curiosity. For what seemed like a sojourn in paradise, I felt her little feet, all six of them, mapping my face's every aspect. Next Smaragdos explored my lip's contour, my chin, my cheeks and temples, and as she did my anger fell away, was forgotten. I returned to the youth that was mine the day I left for the woods with my knobby stick, the same face Beauty would trace with her finger, smiling all the while into my eyes. Just when Smaragdos began her investigation of my right ear, a full pitcher of cold water hit me like a tsunami. Leaping to my feet, I saw the backside of the Novel Plotinus receding in what remained of the light. I would not know until the next day if Smaragdos had escaped in time; she had.

• • •

I once read that a snake will not die a natural death. That murder is the only way it can be made to die. I suppose the same is true of the Plotinus.

• • •

This morning I awakened recalling times past when I would set out at dawn with my knobby stick and meet up with Gazali and the others in front of Fred's. The air sweet with breakfast rolls baking, we'd walk together in silence down Principle Street, turn up Vulgata, and with discretion slip through the bushes onto Plato's Path—named for a man who had lived on that path pulling weeds, eating moss and grass, and overseeing our bird cemetery.

Having reached the bluff, we would stand together tracking the Sun's progress as it surged above Old Bald Head Mountain, illuminating it and the sea. Then each of us would climb our tree. This we would do each day— our way of coping with the taxing demands of life in the city. After an hour, Gazali would break the spell as we all had to get on with our day. He'd say: Good morning everybody! Or: Good morning compatriots! Or even: Good morning my beloveds! When Gazali said this, all of us would begin to chatter like birds.

Recalling this, I find I must do all I can to hold onto it tightly—for the nature of the closet is to cruelly scatter recollections, and what is worse, to infect them with shadows. As today, when during my attempt to return to the past, I thought—despite myself and to my own detriment: But this is how it was before Old Bald Head lost his top (something to do with the Primus' birthday).

. . .

Gazali was our leader—although he would not acknowledge or allow that this was so. We all loved, admired,
and trusted him. He was a master of subversions, a
trickster with a unique genius for hexing the Powers in
effective and inscrutable ways. For example: once when
the Primus was out walking his dog (a gentle and fluffy
mix of Corlu and Proclus), Gazali, with the help of
a drone the size of a fly, managed to attach a vocal-
izer the size of a gnat to the dog's collar so that when-
ever the Primus said a thing, the dog would yelp: *How
stupid is that?*

So venerated was Gazali in our circle that we believed
he could take on the form of a raven at will, that this
was the reason he had not been arrested. He was some-
one of great talent and beauty, and often when we met
together on our rare days of leisure, each one of us
roosting up high in our tree, he would sing to us in such
a way that everything fell into place; the angry clouds,
black as ink, would have scattered and the skies—or so
we imagined—schooled with birds.

The moment I thought of those birds, a sparking of
hornets rocketed through the vent, quickening the air
with their wings. My heart leaping, I searched among
them, hoping to see Smaragdos.

One after another, the hornets overwhelmed the
upper air and scattering, investigated my closet (such as

it is). This scattering was followed by a turnabout and a regrouping so that I next saw only a sphere, rising and soaring, cometic and scintillating, stirring the air with such ardor it grew warmer and warmer, the sphere a sun, spinning as the galaxies spin in their infinite sea of darkness, one sea among an overswarm of seas, in a universe so boundless it cannot be named, for its name alone would take such a number of letters that they would demand a universe to contain them.

Then, in that moment of merging, one hornet lifted herself up and away: it was Smaragdos, of course it was she; I recognized her for the extreme delicacy of her limbs and waist, the intensity of her gaze. Before I could utter her name, she exited the vent like a bullet, vanishing into the mysterious realm whose nature I did not know, vanishing, yet this time I was certain that she would return. Something, I knew it, was about to happen. Something that would dramatically transform my days.

• • •

I awakened thinking Beauty was beside me, that soon we would join the others in the street before setting off in time for the sunrise. I recalled how none of us had ever seen much money; how what we owned we had found on the sidewalks or dumped in the woods. For years Gazali hoarded illicit magazines—illicit as they invariably featured stories devoted to the exodus. Thanks to Gazali's magazines, we knew that people with extravagant fortunes had bought Martian real estate early on and had departed around the time unrest was at its peak. The Plotinus—the first of its kind— made hourly searches, and it was inevitable that sooner or later it would break into Gazali's place, find the magazines and arrest him.

Gazali's magazines contained fantastic images of the Martian landscape, its beauties and asperities, its vistas of tangerine stubble, cerulean ice and turquoise seas; its tsunamis of blue ink and its green dawns. It came as no surprise that the first cities were named Khufu and Khafra, for we saw pyramids with spiraling interiors and obelisks of corrugated glass said to intersect directly with both the Primus and the Cosmos. A massive sphinx had been placed at the crossroads leading from the star port to both cities; the sphinx contained lush gardens, extravagant places to bathe, malls filled with museum plunder. The facades of public buildings featured the Primus' backside, which, in Gazali's words, was indistinguishable from his face. We looked on with amazement as the departures accelerated, vast numbers leaving behind their garbage, their distress and the mansions no one could enter.

It was rumored that there were orchards of quince and mango trees growing within cones of glass, a new kind of telephone tattooed on the wrist, vehicles shaped like shells, surgical implants of unique devices. There were no Martian creatures, yet some insisted they had caught something watching them—from an overhang of ice or uplooking from the turquoise water. The sky the color of a throat.

• • •

Now that I was fully awake and once again alone, I wondered why it is that beauty is offered only to be taken away? Because you are unworthy, I thought I heard the Plotinus bark from behind the air vent. But then Gazali whispered in my ear: For a man to live without beauty is like a fish made to live in the sand.

• • •

Today Smaragdos returned, quickening the hour; having nothing to offer, nor even a drop of water, I gave her my open hand. She alighted as air alights, as dreams alight, and my heart opened as a fist opens when the danger has passed. If once she had mapped my face, now so did she map my hand with her customary delicacy and tenderness. She walked across Pico's fan—that wrinkled terrain between my thumb, Incubus, and first finger, Dolorosa, before acquainting herself with all the others in turn: Torporem, Spiritum, and Interpretandi. Next she examined my wrist, circling it with apparent excitement. Everything that plagued me fell away and I became my lighter self, a self unreachable ever since I stepped out from my front door with my knobby stick—a gesture beyond simplicity, yet foolish beyond belief—and all I loved was taken away. But now I had Smaragdos, making her way from my elbow to the wild woods of my armpit and my chest, exploring the rest of me (what is left of me) before lifting off and away as swift as the wind, to consider my closet's corner across from the air vent, the corner that is the first to receive the Sun's notice. She hovered there for a time. Her behavior reminded me of how Beauty would pace back and forth before deciding on a thing's location. When she had come to her decision, she would nod and before you knew what was happening, a poster would be on the wall, a chair beside the fireplace, a vase of flowers on my desk.

• • •

Had I a lantern, I would spend much less time in the dark.

• • •

All at once and for no apparent reason, I am of a sudden recalling a thing Gazali had read about Mars in one of his contraband magazines that we all found particularly fascinating. Adolescents sent to Mars to procreate were unable to conceive and to this purpose were sequestered in hothouses among a profusion of fruiting plants, pollinated by a clone called a mothwing (it is not a moth) and a bird (perhaps a number of birds) without whose voices newborns cannot survive the first week. These birds feed on a fungus that, allowed to run rife within the hothouses, endangers the mothwing. The birds are raised in auxiliary rooms well-provided with a flower named Ahmad's buttercup (after Ahmad Azari, the first Arabian astronaut). The buttercup depends on a rich soil taken from a forest in what remains of Tunisia. A soil brought to the planet by a fleet of starships. It is possible that none of this is true, but it made sense to me and Gazali. (Why would anyone waste their time inventing such a story as this?)

It was more than the magazines that assured Gazali's arrest. The Plotinus had also located his printer and a stack of flyers, flyers Gazali would post all over the city. It was evident the poor would never make it to Mars. Instead, as Gazali had written on one of his many flyers, flyers that would appear out of nowhere:

THE POOR WILL INHERIT THE EARTH. (Such as it is.)

• • •

Last night I dreamed of the Vector. I saw him as a sage standing from within a many-colored cloud, a cloud made of cotton candy. I saw him as an impostor wearing a cloak of soiled butcher paper held together with tape. On his head he wore a hat made with a pig's liver. I saw him as a butcher wearing a belt studded with knives. He put his hand in his pocket and instead of offering me a breakfast roll, he produced a turd of his own making. I lifted my hand to strike him, but there, in his stead, stood the Vectoress, rising slowly from a pool of honey and fresh water, and she was smiling. Do not forsake yourself, she said tenderly if inscrutably, her face glowing like a bouquet of marigolds.

• • •

All night, memories of Gazali flooded my mind and I could not sleep. I recalled—as I do often—the last afternoon we spent together in his one room stacked with books and magazines—and heard a shattering coming from the street. Running to the window, we saw an absurd and altogether terrifying Plotinus, the size of a bus erect on its hind wheels, rolling our way, informing us that a time of unprecedented ferocity was upon us, that irrelevance was forever silenced, that our purposeless and insignificant bodies would never again clog the system; that lovers would no longer gaze into one another's eyes; that the children of men would not be seen at play on the sidewalks, that the world would shine like polished steel; that the era of the Plotinus had begun.

Those terrible words thundering in our heads, we looked on as quickly approaching, the Plotinus crushed everything in its way—a baker's cart, parked bicycles, random cars, scooters, fire hydrants. We watched as the streets sunk beneath the robot's weight, as the sidewalks lifted and snapped; we heard screams coming from the medical school, the lawyer's office down the street, and seeing smoke rising just a few blocks away, we knew that Fred's was burning.

Somehow I made my way home to Beauty, amazed to see our little house intact. As it happened, that first intrusion of the Plotinus was followed by several months of silence; we had no news, not an inkling as to what would happen next. The morning I set off with my knobby stick was the first time, since the sighting of the Plotinus, that I had stepped out into the street. I do not know what happened to Beauty after, and fear she is lost forever. I cannot think of her without turning to stone.

• • •

Yesterday morning came quickly and in this way I knew it was summer. I had slept so soundly that when I awakened I was startled by the newness of the day, for I had lost all sense of time's passing. I awakened to see a hornet surge into my closet on a granulated beam of light, at once followed by another and yet another; the light and the hornets engulfed the upper air, congregating in the very corner Smaragdos had considered with such intensity the day before. I looked on as they settled briefly on the ceiling and the seam between the walls; as they plotted, or so I thought, an ideal geometrical pattern, each one leaving behind paper scales and fins there where they alighted, only to, in the next instant, take off for the vent, passing those who entered in droves. As I looked on it seemed evident that they were signaling to one another, that if in continual flux they were following a specific trajectory, onrushing, advancing, ascending, descending, crowding together, diverging—only to fall away. I could see that their concentration was total, that a plan was impressed upon their souls, that if at a glance their activity might appear erratic, it was not. In fact, it demonstrated that past, present, and future are not distinct phenomena *but the same thing,* that the hornets' work had been conceived the moment it was completed, or rather, the project had been completed the moment it was conceived. Were they building an apartment house with corridors, hall-ways and a lobby? Or a city with boulevards and avenues? Or might they be at work on a trifecta of palaces? All morning the hornets streamed above me, their bodies propelled through the air vent like meteors, their gestures compelling and precise. Briefly startled, I thought I recognized a schematic plan very like that of the vanished city of Palmanova—a thing I had seen tucked away in Gazali's files. Not much later, unfolding in the twilight, a twilight rich in moonlight, I saw a second level rising above the first—and it recalled the ground plan of what had been the Villa Farannese (a structure also similar to a pharmacy on Mars).

Night came next, the hornets retired as did I, if barely able to contain my excitement. When today the Sun returned, so did the hornets reappear, continuing their work, and a third level was added on. All too briefly I thought I caught a glimpse of a maze of tunneled rooms delicately configured around a public square. (It might have been a ballroom.) Once this addition was complete, a dome—overseen by the large hornet that had recently upended my evening—capped the entire structure. This dome was very like that of a mosque.

• • •

Today I can barely stand, yet I manage to knuckle these words against the vent, taking care to allow the passage of those hornets whose own needs compel their continued, indeed, incessant, comings and goings. Isolated and in this way concealed, I have vowed to continue my story as best I can, with the knowledge—and it is embodied—that I am finite and reaching my limits. If it is true, as the sages say, that all that is below is the mirror of all that is above, then it could be said that nothing escapes concealment. Just as we cannot see the sacred face-to-face, so the sacred is incapable of seeing (and so recognizing) us. Yet, I persist in my thinking that if the Light is visible to us, then we—despite our concealment—are visible to the Light. After all, the Sun and Moon leave their traces within my closet and so within my mind. Given my isolation and impoverishment, I receive the gift of light as a good thing, a thing of power that has demonstrated, again and again, that it is beneficial beyond all else. By descending from the sky into my closet, it is subtle and yet powerful, and always elicits my pleasure. It is because of the light (such as it is) that I am able to see the miraculous hive and those animated creatures housed within, the hive that is in and of itself a talisman and emblematic of the universe. Its presence heals my heart and mind to a great degree. The hive is the most wondrous thing I have ever seen, and Smaragdos (whose return I am awaiting breathlessly), Smaragdos—my winged dragon, my angel, embodies the greatest of wonders, and this brings me to the Beauty who, in a moment of forgetfulness called out, Darling! Do not forget the knobby stick! In that instant of forgetting that the world had shifted on its axis, and its bottom was now on top—so beautiful was the morning, so happy had we been that very hour lounging in each other's arms—she, wanting my safety, decided my fate. In other words, my beloved and I, without intending to, abandoned prudence, we abandoned judgment, and now I am paying for a moment's inattention with my life.

• • •

When I listen to the music the hornets make with their wings, I ascertain that they are in accordance with one another, sharing conversations having to do with domestic requirements, such as the best approach for pillaging the hives of bees, the pantries of the ants. Throughout the day they fly through the vent, back and forth, bringing numerous items lifted from the woods, the city streets, back lots, the public spaces overrun with thorns. I was unable to see just what it was they carried, but I imagined they were filling their pantry with honey from the hidden valley the Vector had once described, and other sweet-smelling things such as yellow amber and the resin of thorny carob.

These thoughts of hives and honey, and the making of things, sent me back to thinking of Mars once again. I imagined that the mall within the sphinx provided refined entertainments and marvelous things to eat formed of the molecules taken from the atmosphere and offered up in fantastical colors, flavors, and shapes. By the afternoon's end, a sudden silence took me by surprise, and I knew the hornets were asleep, one beside the other, like seeds in a husk. And I asked myself, what prevents each and every one from being a messenger of Eros, each and every one, a vessel of love? Seeing this with a terrible clarity within my mind's eye, a clarity unlike any I had known when alive and active in the world, I was overcome, and despite my attempts to hold on, not to succumb to a sorrow all too consuming to survive, I could not help but recall the many nights I slept beside Beauty in a state of grace. Now, in this instant, and from within myself, I fall away, as if in a dream, from a cliff.

• • •

Today in the diffused light of early morning, Smaragdos breached the grid. Before greeting me, she flew to the nest and checked it out from all angles. The nest, perfect and immobile, swelled in the high corner like a fruit from another planet. After she entered a discreet portal to examine the interior, I could hear the touching sound of her little feet making their way in and out of chambers, up and down hallways. When she exited I could tell by the way she moved that she rejoiced in all that she had seen. At once she perched beneath my right eye and gazed upward with such intensity I trembled, for no one had gazed into my eyes since that terrible morning I set off with my knobby stick and left Beauty behind forever. I wished I could offer her a crumb of halva, a drop of water, but perhaps this did not matter as she was otherwise engaged and had already vanished.

I spent the next hour contemplating the nest, imagining what would happen next, what things would be like once her entire community had moved in. Would the sight of them engaging with one another, participating in tasks and events, exacerbate my aloneness or provide entertainment? Relief? Would the nest and its hornets offer a palpable quality of being, an Eros that would illuminate my dark hours?

• • •

I am certain the hornets are individuals, perhaps more authentically so than I am at this moment in time. For I am but parchment and thread. The sound of knuckles rapping on an air vent.

• • •

This evening as I knuckle the vent I gaze at the nest all too aware that despite the fact that I had witnessed its construction from the beginning, still my understanding is an imperfect equivalent of realities within, for such realities are inaccessible (I have no ladder). At any moment now it will be inhabited, and I cannot help but entertain the childish fantasy of making myself so small as to enter the hive's diminutive portal, perhaps even renting an apartment, one with a view of a public park, an orchard or a garden. Then could I live comfortably among the hornets, become acquainted with their ways, their expectations, and, as do they, subsist on stolen honey—a thought that has me salivating like a dog. As I convey these thoughts, a full Moon rises, and I cannot help but notice how the nest attracts the lunar light; it shimmers! If the nest is in the pathway of both the lunar and the solar rays, so then it is in the pathways of the stars, of the entire universe!

If the nest is saturated with light, then must it radiate light and so knowledge of a kind. With time I will within my mind see all that unfolds within the hive. (Or so I would like to think. I realize that there will be no way for me to assure that my assumptions are not simply phantasms.)

• • •

It is my conviction that the nest has a celestial dignity.
If this is so, so it is for all things tangible and intangible.

• • •

Coffee House Press began as a small letterpress operation in 1972 and has grown into an internationally renowned nonprofit publisher of literary fiction, essay, poetry, and other work that doesn't fit neatly into genre categories.

Coffee House is both a publisher and an arts organization. Through our *Books in Action* program and publications, we've become interdisciplinary collaborators and incubators for new work and audience experiences. Our vision for the future is one where a publisher is a catalyst and connector.

LITERATURE
is not the same thing as
PUBLISHING

Funder Acknowledgments

Coffee House Press is an internationally renowned independent book publisher and arts nonprofit based in Minneapolis, MN; through its literary publications and *Books in Action* program, Coffee House acts as a catalyst and connector—between authors and readers, ideas and resources, creativity and community, inspiration and action.

Coffee House Press books are made possible through the generous support of grants and donations from corporations, state and federal grant programs, family foundations, and the many individuals who believe in the transformational power of literature. This activity is made possible by the voters of Minnesota through a Minnesota State Arts Board Operating Support grant, thanks to the legislative appropriation from the Arts and Cultural Heritage Fund. Coffee House also receives major operating support from the Amazon Literary Partnership, Jerome Foundation, Literary Arts Emergency Fund, McKnight Foundation, and the National Endowment for the Arts (NEA). To find out more about how NEA grants impact individuals and communities, visit www.arts.gov.

Coffee House Press receives additional support from Bookmobile; Dorsey & Whitney LLP; Elmer L. & Eleanor J. Andersen Foundation; the Gaea Foundation; the Matching Grant Program Fund of the Minneapolis Foundation; Mr. Pancks' Fund in memory of Graham Kimpton; the Schwab Charitable Fund; and the U.S. Bank Foundation.

The Publisher's Circle of Coffee House Press

Publisher's Circle members make significant contributions to Coffee House Press's annual giving campaign. Understanding that a strong financial base is necessary for the press to meet the challenges and opportunities that arise each year, this group plays a crucial part in the success of Coffee House's mission.

Recent Publisher's Circle members include many anonymous donors, Kathy Arnold, Patricia A. Beithon, Andrew Brantingham, Anitra Budd, Kelli & Dave Cloutier, Mary Ebert & Paul Stembler, Eva Galiber, Jocelyn Hale & Glenn Miller Charitable Fund of the Minneapolis Foundation, William Hardacker, Randy Hartten & Ron Lotz, Dylan Hicks & Nina Hale, Carl & Heidi Horsch, Amy L. Hubbard & Geoffrey J. Kehoe Fund of the St. Paul & Minnesota Foundation, Kenneth & Susan Kahn, the Kenneth Koch Literary Estate, Cinda Kornblum, the Lenfestey Family Foundation, Sarah Lutman & Rob Rudolph, Carol & Aaron Mack, Mary & Malcolm McDermid, Daniel N. Smith III & Maureen Millea Smith, Robin Chemers Neustein, Alan Polsky, Robin Preble, Rebecca Rand, Grant Wood, and Margaret Wurtele.

For more information about the Publisher's Circle and other ways to support Coffee House Press books, authors, and activities, please visit www.coffeehousepress.org/pages/donate or contact us at info@coffeehousepress.org.

Rikki Ducornet is a transdisciplinary artist. Her work is animated by an interest in nature, Eros, tyranny, and the transcendent capacities of the creative imagination. She is a poet, fiction writer, essayist, and artist, and her fiction has been translated into fifteen languages. Her art has been exhibited internationally, most recently with Amnesty International's traveling exhibit *I Welcome*, focused on the refugee crisis. She has received numerous fellowships and awards including an Arts and Letters Award from the American Academy of Arts and Letters, the Charles Flint Kellogg Award in Arts and Letters from Bard College, the Prix Guerlain, and the Lannan Literary Award for Fiction. Her novel *The Jade Cabinet* was a finalist for the National Book Critics Circle Award. She lives in Port Townsend, Washington.

The Plotinus was designed by
Bookmobile Design & Digital Publisher Services.
Text is set in Adobe Caslon Pro.